THE ADVENTU... TOBY DIGZ

THE MIGHTY ARMOR

By DAVID J. HERNANDEZ

Tommy
NELSON®

www.tommynelson.com

A Division of Thomas Nelson, Inc.
www.ThomasNelson.com

For my Mom, Elisabeth.
Thanks for letting me dream!

Text & illustrations copyright © 2003 by David Hernandez

Published in Nashville, Tennessee, by Tommy Nelson®, a Division of Thomas
Nelson, Inc.

Library of Congress Cataloging-in-Publication Data

Hernandez, David, 1964–
   The mighty armor : the adventures of Toby Digz / by David Hernandez.
      p. cm.
   Summary: To escape a spooky night in the treehouse, Toby and Tut
travel through time and find themselves in a Roman jail cell in 60 A.D. with
the apostle Paul, who teaches Toby how to put on the "Armor of God."
   ISBN 1-4003-0196-3 (trade paper)
   [1. Time travel—Fiction. 2. Courage—Fiction. 3. Paul, the Apostle,
Saint—Fiction. 4. Christian life—Fiction. 5. Adventure and adventurers—
Fiction.] I. Title.
PZ7.H43174Mi 2003
[Fic]—dc21

                                                        2003008759

Printed in the United States of America

03 04 05 06 PHX 5 4 3 2 1

Contents

EPOCH 1: Friday!!   1

EPOCH 2: Gearing Up   9

EPOCH 3: The Extreme Outdoors   17

EPOCH 4: Who? Who? Who IS It?   24

EPOCH 5: Tut's Bright Idea   32

EPOCH 6: Go Straight to Jail!   39

EPOCH 7: The Good News   45

EPOCH 8: One Awesome Outfit!   48

EPOCH 9: What a Knight!   53

EPOCH 10: Dragon Breath   57

EPOCH 11: The Dramatic Rescue   63

EPOCH 12: A Royal Celebration   68

EPOCH 13: The Armor of God   75

EPOCH 14: Explore More!   81

The Armor of God   86

Digzig   87

Digz-tionary   88

DigzGear   89

Let's Draw Tut   90

EPOCH 1
Friday!!

"Friday at last!"
Toby cheered as
he jumped off
the school bus
and onto his
Duneripper.
What a crummy
week! Charlie
had been making
everyone's life
miserable.
Vrooommm!!!
Toby zoomed to his mailbox
to see if the latest issue of *Explore More!*
had arrived. He peered in:
empty again!

Rrrrff . . . flip
the pages and
watch me climb!

"Maybe tomorrow," Lauren called from across the street.

"Yeah," Toby mumbled but then tried to smile at his friend, remembering *her* day yesterday.

Poor Lauren! Charlie had made her lose the homeschooling spelling bee at the library last night. When it was her turn, Charlie shot a spitball at her head, and Lauren spelled "p-e-s-t" instead of "p-e-a-s-a-n-t." Charlie cackled like a chicken! For months, Lauren had been the top speller in her group.

With Tut at his heels, Toby zipped into his house, tossed his book bag onto the hallway desk, and strolled into the kitchen where his mother was preparing BROCCOLI!! Blech!

"How was school, Toby?" she asked.

"Other than Charlie's stunts, okay," he said and showed his mom the sketch of the **solar system** he had drawn for her.

"Verrry nice!" She smiled, hanging it on the fridge.

"So, Mom . . ." Toby began casually, "tonight, the planet **Venus** should shine brighter than the other planets."

"Really?" she asked, handing four plates to Toby.

Toby began setting the table. "Yeah! I was wondering . . . may I sleep in the tree house tonight?" he asked hopefully.

"Well, I don't know . . . ," she stalled. "I suppose, but take Tut."

"Awesome!" Toby shouted.

Suddenly, broccoli didn't seem so bad!

EPOCH 2
Gearing Up

After wolfing down some broccoli-chicken casserole, two glasses of milk, and a slice of chocolate cake, Toby dashed up to his bedroom. Time to pack! He reviewed the gear he would need:

> **Radcom** ✓
> **Gleembeam** ✓
> **Jampak** ✓
> **Gloomgogz** . . .

Just then, Toby's Radcom began to squeal.

"Arrr ruf!" Tut barked at the blaring radio.

"*chhksksrssst* . . . Come in Digz Seven . . . *chhzst* . . . This is Windy Zero. Come in!"

Toby grabbed the Radcom and pressed the button. "This is Digz Seven. I read you, loud and clear, Windy Zero. Go ahead."

Charlie's voice was muffled. "Wanna hang out with me, Lauren, and Rosetta, tomorrow? I found a huge box in my garage and my dad said I could have it. I'm turning it into a **fortress**! It's going to be WAY cooler than that pile of boxes in your tree house."

Toby couldn't believe Rosetta would even talk to Charlie after he freed the science rat in her desk on Tuesday. She had almost fainted! And Lauren? She cried in the bathroom for 30 minutes after losing the spelling bee. Boy!!!

"Hey! Earth to Toby! Are you coming tomorrow or not?" Charlie demanded.

Ugh! Charlie was really in a mood
these days. Toby wondered if he
would try to scare him that night.
He was probably just trying to get
under his skin.

   Toby scanned his room one last
time for anything he'd forgotten.
Then, he and Tut took the stairs two
at a time.

   Neither noticed the batteries that
bounced out of Toby's Jampak.

EPOCH 3

The Extreme Outdoors

Timmy, Toby's little brother, was playing video games in the den when Toby came running through. He heard Toby's batteries hit the stairs and called after him, "I think you dropped—"

"Gotta go!" Toby interrupted. "We're on a mission!" he yelled, the door slamming behind him.

Timmy shrugged and set the batteries on the table, then went back to conquering the little, green men in the ninth level of Martian Invaders III.

Outside, Toby climbed up to his tree house and flipped the switch to lower the **Doggy-vator**. Tut's tail was wagging all the way up.

"This is it!" Toby said, scratching Tut's back. "Tonight, we face the backyard, the wilderness, the frontier, the EXTREME OUTDOORS!!!"

SPACE

"Woof!" Tut held his head high and gave Toby a big, wet lick on the cheek.

Toby twisted the telescope onto its stand, rolled out his **astronomy** chart, and poured fresh milk into Tut's bowl. "That should do it. All systems are go!" Toby said.

He and Tut sat back on the pile of pillows and shared a bag of Zippy Chips.

"I still can't believe Lauren and Rosetta are playing with Charlie after the way he acted this week!" Toby griped. Tut raised an eyebrow.

The sun was sinking behind the trees in the field just beyond Toby's backyard. Suddenly, the Radcom squealed again. Toby and Tut jumped off the pillows!

"Digz Seven? This is Daddy Digz One. You guys okay out there?" The Radcom gave another squeal.

"Just fine, Dad!" Toby replied in his bravest voice.

"Be sure to call if you get sca—um, I mean, if you need anything," he offered. "Daddy Digz One, over and out!"

"You got it, Dad! Good night," answered Toby.

"Look, Tut!" Toby pointed to the sky. "It's getting dark enough to see the stars."

Tut stretched his front legs to the window sill. The stars beamed. The whole neighborhood was visible from high in the tree house.

Toby adjusted his telescope: a little twist to the left, a half-turn to the right. "Wow!" he shouted, "I can see the **craters** on the moon!"

Tut was too busy watching a cat scurry up the tree beside them.

"HISSSSSSS!!" The cat spotted Tut. Tut replied with several fierce barks, warning the cat to scram.

"What's the matter, boy?" Toby asked in a squeaky voice. "Something out there? . . . Maybe I *should* be afraid," he whispered. "Maybe Charlie was right."

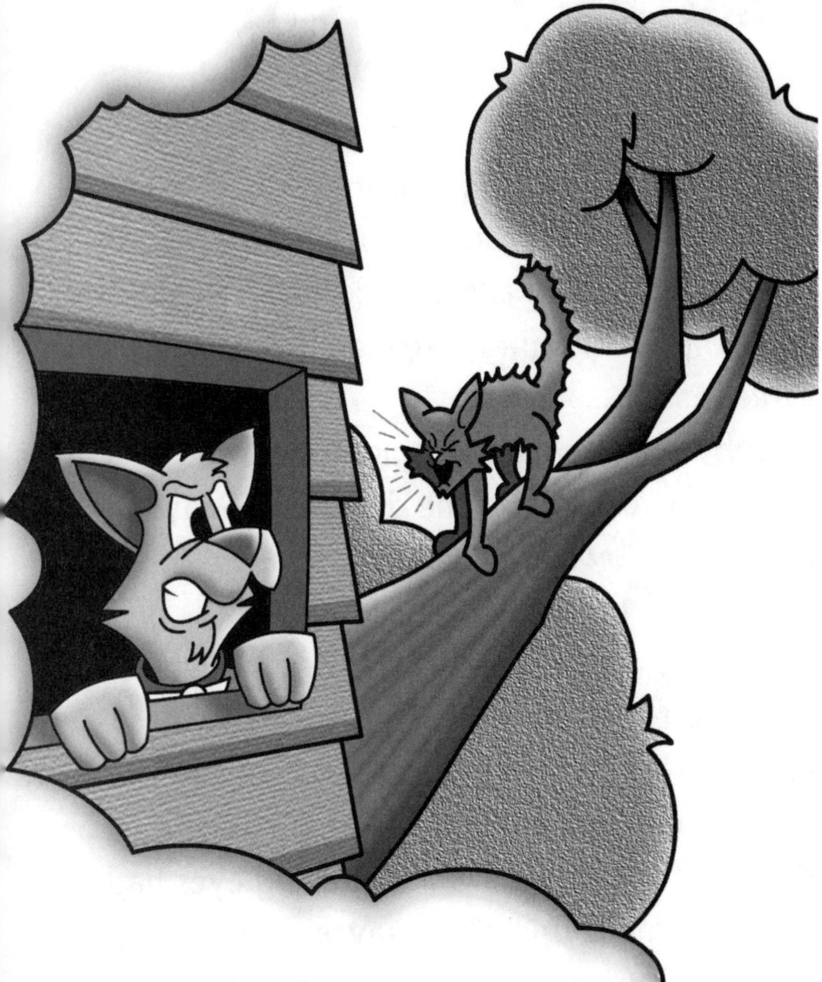

EPOCH 4

Who? Who? Who IS it?

Toby looked out to see what was bothering Tut, but the cat was long gone.

Toby had never looked out into the woods at night. He put his arm around Tut. "It's okay, boy. There's nothing out there." Just then— *screeeech!!!*

Toby quickly scanned the trees. Two glowing eyes pierced the darkness. "Maybe an owl?" Toby suggested.

"Arrrk," Tut whined.

"What? What is it, boy?!" Toby looked to Tut for an answer. "Oh, sorry," Toby loosened the grip he had around Tut's neck.

Toby pulled out his Gleembeam and shined it toward where the glowing eyes had been. Hmm, nothing but leaves now.

"For security measures!" he said, leaving the Gleembeam on the table next to them.

Toby went back to looking through his telescope, but he couldn't keep from glancing at the shadowy trees. The branches swayed and the wind rustled the leaves.

Tut yawned and curled up on the pillows. "Go ahead. Take a nap. I'll keep a lookout," Toby told him.

SCCRRAAATCH!! Something scraped the roof of the tree house. "Just a branch," Toby assured a snoring Tut.

"Charlie—that better not be you!" he called in his deepest voice. Charlie had thrown a water balloon at Toby on Monday. It had ruined the watercolor painting he'd made in art class that day. "I wouldn't put anything past him," Toby muttered, turning back to his telescope.

Suddenly, the Gleembeam flickered. Toby leaped to grab it, but it slowly dimmed and then flickered out completely.

"Rats!" Toby fumbled around in the darkness. He whistled for Tut to fetch his Jampak.

Tut opened one eye, then both, stretched, and slowly dragged the pack to Toby.

"Good boy!" Toby patted Tut's back while he rummaged through the gear.

Toby moaned. "I'm sure I packed extra batteries, but they're not here!" He could barely see Tut sitting right next to him.

"Tut, can you help me find the Radcom?" Toby was trying to remain calm. "Dad will bring us new batteries."

They began to search for the Radcom, when they noticed that the glowing eyes had returned. *HOOOOOT!!!*

Toby jumped back and bumped the table where the Radcom sat. The Radcom wobbled, then bounced right into Tut's bowl of milk and sank with a gurgle.

Toby blindly continued his search. He stopped and pulled Tut close. "I guess I'm not all *that* brave," he whispered.

EPOCH 5

Tut's Bright Idea

Sluuuurp! Tut licked Toby's cheek, then bit onto his shirt and tugged him toward the hanging blankets and boxes that formed Toby's makeshift cave.

"You're a genius, Tut!" Toby cried. "We'll be safe in the Bible!"

Relieved, Toby slung his Jampak over his shoulders, pulled Tut to his side, closed his eyes, and yelled:

"LET'S DIG INTO THE BIBLE!"

Toby opened his eyes. The hanging blankets had transformed into . . . into . . . stone walls??? Toby said a short prayer as he shivered from a sudden chill, "Please help me be strong . . ."

Toby reached into his Jampak and pulled out his Gloomgogz. He could see much better with night-vision. He looked around. They were behind thick, steel bars. On the other side of the bars was a snoring guard.

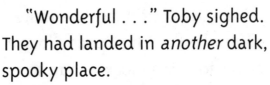

"Wonderful . . ." Toby sighed. They had landed in *another* dark, spooky place.

Tut just whined, staring into the corner of the room.

"What is it, boy?" Toby turned to see a man sitting beneath a small window. The moonlight shone on the man's face.

"Well, hello there, little fellow," the man said as Tut ran over and licked his hand.

"Beautiful night, huh?" the man asked Toby, pointing toward the window. "The stars are so bright!"

"I noticed that too," Toby said.

The man continued to admire the stars. Toby pulled out his **Epoch Clock** and pushed the button. The clock began to glow, and the antenna popped up. It read:

ROME ◆ A.D. 60 ◆ SPRING ◆ 8:00 P.M.

"Whooaa . . ." Toby said under his breath.

"By the way, I am Paul," the man told Toby and Tut.

EPOCH 6
Go Straight to Jail!

"So, what strange deed brings you to this place?" Paul asked Toby.

"We were looking for a safe place, but it's creepier in here than in my tree house at night! We're in jail, right?"

"Yes." Paul chuckled and motioned for Toby and Tut to come sit beside him. Tut curled up next to Paul, as if he'd known him forever.

Toby looked around. "Aren't *you* afraid here all alone?"

Paul smiled. "Ahh, but I am *not* alone, my young friend!"

Tut began to sniff around for others.

"God is right here, right now," Paul said. "He is with us wherever we go, no matter what!"

". . . w-what . . . What?" the guard mumbled as he stirred from his slumber. Quickly, Toby strapped on his **Dashpads**, grabbed Tut, and jumped up to the bars on the window. He clung to the bars, not making a sound.

The guard stretched, yawned, and walked over to Paul's cell. The guard rubbed his eyes and scanned the jail cell. "I thought I heard voices!" Paul just smiled at the guard.

Tut began to wiggle, and Toby's grip began to give.

"Hmmph!" the guard mumbled and marched away.

"Whew!" Toby let out a deep breath and quietly lowered himself and Tut to the floor. "Close call!" he whispered to Paul.

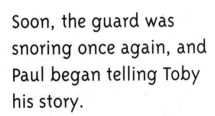

The Good News

Soon, the guard was snoring once again, and Paul began telling Toby his story.

"Before, everyone called me Saul. I was not a happy man, and I wasn't liked very much either. I would arrest people just for believing in Jesus," he told Toby.

"Really?" Toby asked, raising an eyebrow.

"Yes, but one day, Jesus appeared to me and showed me that I had been wrong. He changed my name to Paul and asked me to help share the Good News with the entire world: God loves everyone!" Paul explained.

"That's a big job!" Toby said excitedly.

"Yes. That's why I'm in this prison right now—for the same reason 'Saul' would put people in jail," Paul explained. "However, I've learned that God is always watching, and He will always protect you," Paul said.

Toby looked a little unsure. "What about when you're in your tree house and there's a 'SCRRRIIITCH' and a 'HOOOOT' outside and your flashlight goes dead?"

Paul laughed. "Well, you just have to put on the **Armor** of God and face whatever it is that is scaring you."

Toby leaped to his feet. "The *Armor of God?* What's that?"

"I can teach you," Paul told him.

"But can you teach me how to *wear* the Armor of God?" Toby asked.

"I think you'll figure *that* out on your own." Paul smiled.

EPOCH 8

One Awesome Outfit!

"Before you arrived, I was writing a letter," Paul told Toby. "In it, I was explaining the Armor of God. I think it will help you understand how to wear the Armor. Would you like me to read it?"

"Please!" Toby shouted.

Paul cleared his throat:

Be strong with the Lord's mighty power. Use every piece of God's armor.

Stand your ground, putting on the sturdy belt of truth and the body armor of God's **righteousness**.

For shoes, put on the boots of peace that come from the good news, so that you will be prepared.

In every battle, you will need faith as your shield.

Put on **salvation** as your helmet and take the sword of the Word of God. Pray at all times.

"WOW! That's one awesome outfit!" Toby exclaimed. "With the mighty Armor of God, I could be brave—just like Joshua when he led the battle of Jericho! Or as strong as Samson when he pushed over the giant pillars of stone!"

Paul just smiled.

Toby realized that God had been with him all along in his tree house. "I don't have to be scared anymore! I can just put on the Armor of God! Thanks, Paul!"

"Hey, I got something for *you*," Toby told Paul and pulled a bag of Zippy Chips from his Jampak. Tut drooled as he watched Paul take a chip from the bag.

"These are veeery tasty!" Paul said.

"Woof! Woof!" Tut agreed. He sat, rolled over, and begged, hoping one of his tricks would score a chip.

"Oh, okay, boy," Paul said, laughing as he tossed Tut a chip.

Early the next morning, Toby told Paul good-bye. "I guess we've got to get back to the tree house now," he explained.

Paul waved to Toby. "Bye. And pray for me as I try to spread the Good News!" Paul said.

"Oh, I will!" Toby answered.

EPOCH 9
What a Knight!

Toby and Tut stood back in the corner of the
jail where they had entered. They closed
their eyes, and in a blink, they were once
again surrounded by the blankets of Toby's
tree house cave.

Immediately they heard girls' voices:
"Heeelp! Heeelp! Someone save us!"

Toby and Tut crawled out of the
cave, jumped onto the Doggy-vator, and
Toby hit the switch. Down they flew.

Toby ran to the side yard and looked over the bushes into Charlie's backyard.

It was Lauren and Rosetta screaming! They looked like they were being held captive! Charlie stood laughing nearby. Toby quickly scaled the fence while Tut leaped over the bushes.

Charlie stood on a big cardboard box. "If you think Charlie is MEAN, wait until you meet the wrath of KING Charlie!" he yelled at Lauren and Rosetta.

"Ooohhh, Toby!" Rosetta screeched, "We are beautiful princesses and we've been captured by the mean ol' King Charlie of Charlestown! Help us, Toby! Help us!"

"I will save you!" Toby declared.

"Arrr Ruf Ruf!" Tut ran back and forth in front of the girls.

"Tut, you will be my faithful steed. And I will be the mighty **knight**, Sir Toby!"

Just then, King Charlie leaped down from his fortress. "We'll see about that, *Sir* Toby. How brave will you be when you meet the mighty Behemoth?!"

EPOCH 10

Dragon Breath

"King Charlie's dragon breathes FIRE!"
Princess Lauren quickly informed Sir Toby.
"Dragon?" Sir Toby asked fearlessly.
"I fear no dragon."

"DRAGON!!" the princesses both screamed as Behemoth swooshed down from the sky toward them, exposing his green teeth dripping with dragon drool.

"Phew!" Princess Lauren held her nose as the dragon opened its mouth wide.

"Please, Sir Toby, SAVE US!" Princess Rosetta cried out.

"Have no fear! I shall obey the Code of **Chivalry**!" Sir Toby exclaimed.

"The coat of shivery?" Princess Rosetta tilted her head and looked at Lauren.

"It's *code* for 'I'm a scaredy cat!'" King Charlie laughed.

"Ahem—actually, chivalry is the promise a knight makes to treat everyone with respect, to *help* anyone in need, and to be brave, honest, and loyal at all times," Sir Toby answered.

"Oh, how charming!" Princess Rosetta giggled.

"Bleeecckk!!" the king gagged.

"Chivalry sounds cool," Princess Lauren agreed. "It's kind of how Jesus wants us to be, too."

"Whatever—can we just get on with this?" The king was getting bored with all this talk of respect and honor.

Sir Toby called his steed to his side and said, "I shall put on the Armor of God to face Behemoth!"

The Body of Righteousness!

The Belt of Truth!

The Boots of Peace!

The Shield of Faith!

The Helmet of Salvation!

*And the Sword of the Spirit,
which is the Word of God!*

Sir Toby stood tall, as the sun reflected off of his new Armor.

EPOCH 11

The Dramatic Rescue

Sir Toby watched Behemoth fly back up into the sky, then swoop down again, aiming right at him. He grabbed the ledge of the fortress wall just in time to swing up and onto the back of the fierce dragon.

"Giddy-up!" he yelled.

Behemoth flew high into the sky flipping over and over, trying to make Toby fall off. Toby slipped down its back and grabbed its tail. Feeling Toby grab on, the dragon whipped its tail, and Toby went spinning toward the ground.

"Aaahhh!!!" Sir Toby yelled as he crashed onto the roof of King Charlie's fortress. He looked at King Charlie and grinned. "It's a good thing I have the Helmet of Salvation!"

"Look what you did, you creep!" Charlie yelled, giving Toby a slight shove.

"Hey! I was getting eaten by *your* dragon!" Toby shot back.

"Behemoth, go get the princesses!" King Charlie yelled.

Again, Behemoth soared toward the girls, his giant wings flapping in the air. Toby knew he had to save the girls—and quick! He whistled for his trusty steed.

Tut's ears perked up as Toby called, "Remember, Tut, God is always protecting us!" Together, they galloped to where the girls were held captive.

"Sir Toby! Look out behind you!" Princess Lauren shouted.

Toby turned just in time to see the massive dragon soaring down with its mouth wide open.

Rooooaaaar!!!

Sir Toby raised his sword high into the air and shouted, "I have the Sword of the Spirit because I know the Word of God!"

The creature blasted gigantic flames from its mouth, as Tut pulled the girls to safety. They all ran until they could no longer see the dragon.

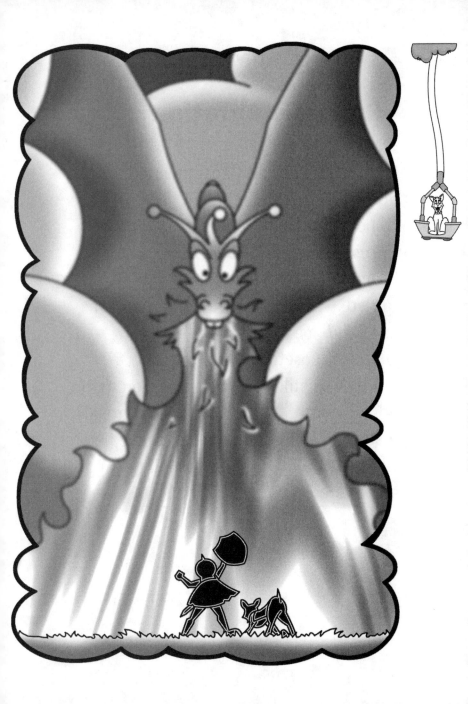

EPOCH 12

A Royal Celebration

"My heroes!" Princess Rosetta cried, hugging Sir Toby and Tut.

"I didn't know you were a knight!" Princess Lauren said to Toby.

"Actually, I'm not a knight yet," Toby giggled. "To be a knight, a royal person has to *dub* me."

"Dub?" Rosetta asked.

Toby was still watching for King Charlie and Behemoth. "*Dubbing* is when a royal person taps the shoulders of a brave hero. Once he is dubbed, he is officially a knight!" he answered.

"Oh, Sir Toby! You are so brave. I am sure you will become a true knight!" Princess Rosetta exclaimed and kissed Toby's cheek.

"This isn't over yet!" King Charlie yelled as he came running toward them. "You cannot free the princesses! I'm King Charlie! And no one is more powerful!"

"Okay, okay, Charlie. Calm down. We're *just* playing . . . remember?" Toby said.

Princess Rosetta took off her cape and placed it around Sir Toby. Princess Lauren took Toby's sword and tapped his shoulders with it. "I *dub* thee, Sir Toby of Digztown, brave hero and man of God!"

Just then, Charlie pushed between Toby and Lauren and shouted right in Toby's face, "I *dub* thee, Sir Doofus of Doofustown, wanna-be hero and friend to wimpy dogs and stupid girls!"

"Real funny, Charlie," Toby said and turned away.

But Charlie kept on. "Ooooo, look at me! I'm soooooo brave. I can spend the night in my tree house with my *big, bad* puppy!"

"You're so mean!" Rosetta said to Charlie.

"And I don't see anything special about his clothes! Oh, wait! They are kind of HOLEY!" Charlie burst into another fit of laughter.

EPOCH 13
The Armor of God

Toby and the gang rested under the tree. "Hey, we can start a new game," Toby suggested.

"I wouldn't play with you nerds if I *had* to," Charlie said walking toward his house.

"Fine then, Charles! Suit yourself," Lauren said.

Everyone but Charlie plopped down on the grass beneath a tree to plan their next adventure. A little while later, Charlie came back out and climbed into the tree.

"Oh, I know! We can be beautiful princesses waiting for our Prince Charming to come and rescue us," Rosetta suggested, winking at Toby.

"Sounds like what we just played," Toby said, looking up into the tree for Charlie. Just then he spotted a large, green water balloon directly over them.

Then, it dawned on Toby—the Armor of God wasn't for fighting imaginary dragons; it was meant for situations just like this one! From now on, the Armor of God could help Toby face Charlie's tricks.

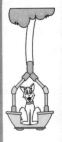

"Run!" Toby yelled to the girls. They all scrambled just in time for the balloon to splat on the ground, sending water splashing in every direction.

"I wear the mighty Armor, and as long as God is with me, I have nothing to fear," Toby said as he lifted the Shield of Faith. "You might be able to hit me with water balloons and spitballs, but your insults bounce right off me!" Toby yelled.

"Oh yeah?" Charlie called. "You're just a girly PRINCESS like Rosetta and Lauren!"

"That's totally lame, Charlie. Why don't you just stop so we can be friends again?" Toby said.

"Wow! That Armor really works!" Rosetta said.

"Very BIG of you, Toby. I'm impressed," Lauren said.

Charlie thought for a minute, then climbed down out of the tree and joined them.

EPOCH 14
Explore More!

"So," Charlie, "can the Armor of God *really* help you with things—like when you're afraid or when you wanna stand up to people who bother you?"

"Yup!" Toby said.

"That's pretty cool . . ." Charlie said under his breath.

"Will you teach *us* about the Armor of God? Huh, Toby? Will you?" Rosetta jumped up and down.

Lauren smiled. "I bet *I* know where you learned about the Armor."

"HEY! Did you go into your cave without us?" asked Charlie.

"Yup!" Toby said again.

"Awww . . . you should've taken us!" Charlie said. "Even though I haven't exactly been your *best* friend this week, will you still teach me about the Armor?" Charlie asked sheepishly.

"Don't do it, Toby!" Rosetta whined. "Charlie will be an even BIGGER bully if he has ARMOR!"

Lauren smiled. "Don't worry, Rosy. I don't think he could use it *that* way!"

"Sure, I'll teach you," Toby said. "What are friends for! Besides, I think you're really going to need it!"

Toby and the girls giggled.

"What's so funny?" Charlie asked.

"Hey, what's Tut doing?" Rosetta asked.

They all turned to see Tut growling and chewing on Charlie's box. He gave it a shake and began pulling it all around the backyard.

"Well, duh!" Charlie smirked. "He's 'dragon' the box!"

Just then, the postman pulled up to Toby's house. From the side yard, Toby recognized the unmistakable silver envelope in the postman's hands.

"It's here!!!" Toby shouted and ran to grab *Explore More!* before it could hit the mailbox.

The End

THE ARMOR OF GOD

In the days of old, brave, honest warriors protected the land. These were the knights.

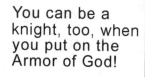

You can be a knight, too, when you put on the Armor of God!

Helmet
(salvation)

Body
(righteousness)

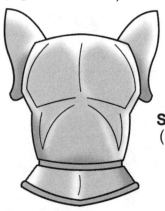

Shield
(faith)

Sword
(spirit)

Boots
(peace)

Belt
(truth)

And did you know that a knight's glove is called a **gauntlet**?

DIGZIG

TOBY'S SECRET PICTURE WRITING

Toby made up his own picture writing, just like the hieroglyphs the Egyptians used. Use this page to translate the secret messages Toby has hidden in this book!

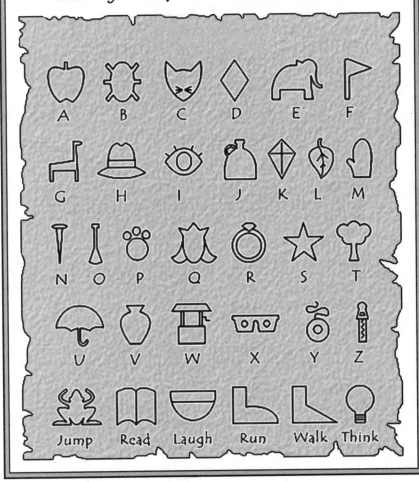

DIGZ-TIONARY

Armor (AR-mer)
Protective clothing, usually made of metal.

Astronomy (uh-STRON-uh-me)
The science dealing with the universe
beyond the earth.

Chivalry (SHIV-ul-ree)
A knight's code of honesty. A respectful
way to act toward others.

Crater (KRAY-tur)
A cup-shaped cavity in the earth or other
heavenly body.

Fortress (FOR-triss)
A large building, fort, or castle.

Knight (nite)
An honest and brave warrior who helps
anyone he meets. Many knights lived in
the Middle Ages (A.D. 500 to A.D. 1500).

Righteousness (RIE-chess-ness)
Doing what is right and honorable.

Salvation (sal-VAY-shin)
The saving of a person from sin.

Solar System (SO-ler SIS-tim)
The sun and all of the planets in its orbit.

Venus (VEE-niss)
The second planet from the sun in our
solar system.

DIGZ GEAR

GLOOMGOGZ
Night-vision goggles

EPOCH CLOCK
Time and space sensor

RADCOM
Radio
communicator

GLEEMBEAM
Flashlight

DOGGY-VATOR
Tut's treehouse basket

JAMPAK
Toby's backpack

DASHPADS
High-flying jump boots

DUNERIPPER
4-wheeling skateboard

Check out all of the DigzGear online at www.tobydigz.com

LET'S DRAW

TUT

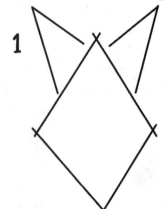

1 Draw one diamond, and add two triangles.

2 Now draw these circles.

3 Next draw the nose and mouth triangles, the collar, ear, and hair lines.

4 Then finish up the drawing.

KEEP PRACTICING!

Fantastical adventure and biblical fact in an all-new series for young readers.

With a little help from their imaginations, Toby and his friends crawl through the makeshift cave in his tree house to find an ancient world of adventure. As Toby and the gang journey back in time, they meet major Bible heroes and learn—up close and personal—about the culture and history of biblical times.

Cutting-edge art paired with stories of fantastical adventure and biblical fact make the all-new Toby Digz series a must-have for young readers. Kids will relate to Toby's predicaments and his quirky sense of humor. Parents will love the Bible stories and biblical truths woven throughout these tales of adventure.